P9-BIJ-407

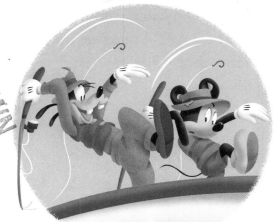

Gone Fishing!

Adapted by Sherri Stoner

Based on the episode by Kim Duran

Illustrated by the Disney Storybook Art Team

 A GOLDEN BOOK • NEW YORK

ISBN 978-0-7364-3844-5 (trade) — ISBN 978-0-7364-3799-8 (ebook)
Printed in the United States of America
10 9 8 7 6 5 4 3 2 1

Mickey and Goofy are getting ready for their annual fishing trip.

"Hot dog, Goofy! It's gonna be just you and me and all the fish in Hot Dog Lake," Mickey says.

"Yep! Nothing but Goofy and Mickey buddy time!" Goofy replies. "I'll teach you my special sidewinder-loop deluxe fishing cast."

Minnie and Daisy give the fellas a picnic lunch. Donald rushes over with sunscreen.

"Don't forget this— **WAKK!**" He trips and squeezes the sunscreen all over his beak.

"I think you're covered," Cuckoo-Loca says.

Mickey and Goofy drive off as the rest of the gang waves goodbye.

Minnie sighs. "Gee, relaxing by the lake sounds divine."

"So does eating those sammies," Cuckoo-Loca says dreamily.

"And catching fish!" Donald adds.

As Daisy, Donald, and Cuckoo-Loca settle down to read, Minnie comes up with a great idea.

"Let's join Mickey and Goofy!" she says.

Goofy has just started teaching Mickey his special fishing technique when Donald zooms up in his roadster and the girls arrive in the Happy Helpers van. Mickey and Goofy exchange glances. They were not expecting visitors!

Donald heads right out onto the lake and looks for fish on his sonar screen.

"**WAK!** What a whopper!" he shouts when he spots a huge fish. He quickly shoots a hook into the water with his high-tech fishing rod.

Back onshore, Mickey and Goofy have finally finished
helping the girls unpack. But as they reach for their fishing
rods, Minnie and Daisy hand them badminton rackets.

"You worked so hard helping us, you deserve a relaxing
game of badminton!" Minnie says.

"Girls against boys! Game on!" Cuckoo-Loca announces.

Just then, Donald gets a bite. He reels it in, but there's just a boot on the end of his line. He shakes the fishing pole, crying, "Shoo, boot!" and the rod slips out of his hands and sinks into the water.

Donald quickly makes himself a new rod with a mop. He uses a sandwich for bait and gets right back to fishing.

As soon as Donald dangles the sandwich over the water, a huge fish pops up and grabs on to it. "Gotcha!" Donald yells. Suddenly, he's pulled out of the boat as the fish swims away. **"Whooaaa!"**

Meanwhile, the badminton game has ended, and Goofy and Mickey are finally ready to start fishing. But Minnie points to the lake.

"Look at Donald go!" she says.

"He's caught **a whopper**!" says Daisy.

"Looks like the whopper caught *him*," Cuckoo-Loca says.

The huge fish drags Donald straight toward a diving platform.

"WAAK! I'm a goner!" he yells. The platform tilts like a ramp, sending Donald soaring into the air. "Heeellllp!"

Mickey and Goofy jump into their boat and zoom off to rescue their friend.

"Hold still, will ya?"
Goofy hollers.

"Tell that to the fish!"
Donald squawks back.

Cuckoo-Loca tells the others that the fish is dragging Donald toward Danger Cove.

"Why do they call it that?" Minnie asks.

"Probably because it leads to **Danger Falls**," Cuckoo-Loca replies.

"Danger Falls?" scream Daisy and Minnie at the same time.

They quickly jump into Donald's cabin cruiser so they can warn the boys.

But Donald, Mickey, and Goofy are already aware of the danger.

Mickey has an idea to keep Donald from going over the falls. "Can you reach him with your special sidewinder-loop deluxe fishing cast?" he asks Goofy.

"I think we'll both have to snag him," says Goofy. "Ready for your lesson?"

"It's finally fishing time, good buddy!" Goofy continues. "Here's what ya do: pull back, thumb the reel, tap your toe three times, twist, swivel, pivot, round and round she goes, and let her fly!"

Their lines zip out at the same time and hook Donald's shirt. **"Hot dog, we did it!"** says Mickey.

They reel Donald in and he grabs on to their boat. Now the huge fish is dragging all three of them toward Danger Falls!

"We've got to cut the whopper loose!" Mickey hollers.

"Wait! Not yet!" cries Donald as he pulls out his phone and takes a selfie with his catch. "Okay, now you can cut the line."

Goofy gets a snapping turtle from the water.
When the turtle chomps the line, Donald flies
up and over the boat. Luckily, the girls catch
him in a fishing net.

"Thanks, everyone. **What a ride!**"
Donald says.

Donald, Daisy, Minnie, and Cuckoo-Loca are ready for more fun with the whole gang.

"Well, actually, we were hoping for some quality Goofy and Mickey buddy time," Goofy says nicely.

"We like being with all of you," Mickey starts. "It's just . . ."

"Sorry for forcing a group outing on you," Minnie says. "We know how important it is for friends to spend time together."

Donald and the girls head to shore in his cabin cruiser.

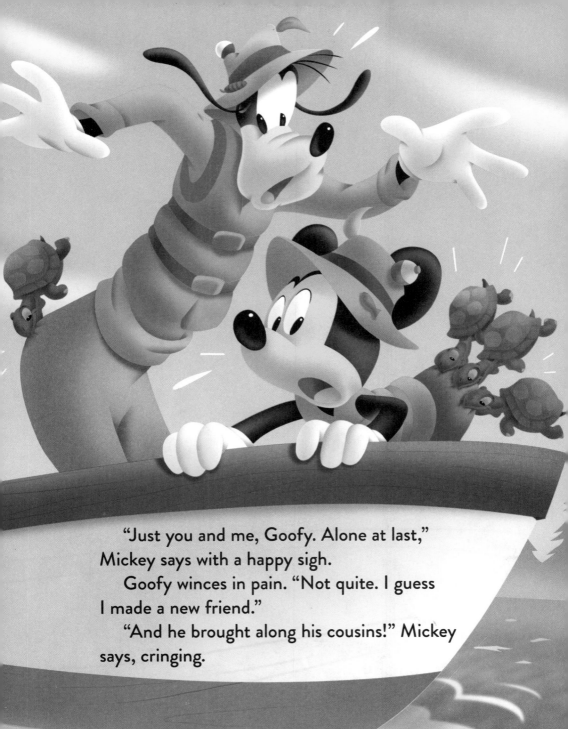

"Just you and me, Goofy. Alone at last," Mickey says with a happy sigh.

Goofy winces in pain. "Not quite. I guess I made a new friend."

"And he brought along his cousins!" Mickey says, cringing.

"Yeoooow-hoowww-hooooie!"
"Aww, sounds like Goofy and Mickey's buddy time is going great!" Minnie says.